Joshua's Amazing Gift

Go where your song guides you ™

By Dietrich Thompson

Illustrated by Randy Knoble

A sample of the songs integrated into this story can be heard at dietrichthompson.com

Interactive eBook versions of this story can also be discovered through dietrichthompson.com

Special thanks to
Elisabeth Thompson, Delano Thompson, Alexander Thompson,
Mary and Dan Riordan, Wil Knoble and Terra Knoble.

Joshua laid on his bed trying to come up with an amazing gift for Rob, his older brother. Today is Rob's birthday and Joshua hadn't gotten him a present yet. Joshua thought, "I should see what others are going to give Rob."

On his way downstairs, Joshua smelled his Grandma's famous 7-up pound cake. When he entered the kitchen he began to sing his Grandma's favorite song, "*Smelled your good cooking when I walked through the door. Even with my eyes closed, I know what I know. I am home, Grandma I'm home, I am home, Grandma I'm home.*" Grandma's smile grew wider as Joshua's voice filled the kitchen.

After singing, Joshua said, "Grandma, I need an amazing gift for Rob's birthday, but I don't know what to do. What should I give him?" Grandma told him she baked Rob's favorite cake. Then Grandma smiled and said, "Maybe you should give him something that will make you both happy."

Next, Joshua ran into his Mom and Dad's bedroom just as they were putting a bow on his brother's gift. Joshua asked excitedly, "What did you get him?" His Mom whispered, "It's a new basketball."
"Wow!" yelled Joshua.

Joshua immediately broke into an old song he'd heard his mom and dad sing when they played basketball with Rob every Friday night. *"Every Friday, me and family we play basketball and we really don't know who's going to win."* Joshua's parents loved to hear him sing because it always made the family so happy.

Then Joshua ran into the Garage to see his sister Zoe and Arvind, Rob's best friend. They were listening to a new song on the radio. Joshua liked the song; so he joined in. *"All the party people on the on the dance floor, they want to dance a little more. Won't you, dance to, my groove, dance to, dance to my groove."* Soon everyone was dancing to the song. Zoe said, "Joshua, you make music so much fun!"

After the song Zoe wrapped a T-shirt she'd made all by herself. It had a picture of Rob's favorite basketball team on it. Arvind proudly displayed a poster of their favorite basketball team. "Wow," said Joshua. "Those are cool gifts." "Everyone has great ideas but me," thought Joshua.

Joshua went back to his bedroom to do some serious thinking. He remembered how Rob always grinned when he sang. Joshua decided his gift would be a song for Rob, so he made a little song in his head. After practicing Joshua signed Rob's birthday card, which had a funny joke about basketball players on it.

That afternoon at the birthday party Joshua couldn't wait to get a hunk of his Grandma's famous cake. Soon it was time to sing Happy Birthday. Joshua's voice soared as he sang "Happy Birthday!" Singing was the only time Mom allowed him to use what she called his "Outside voice" inside the house.

After the song, everyone gave Rob his gifts. He loved all
of them. When he read Joshua's card he laughed so
hard that he fell out his chair!

Then, Joshua told Rob he made a song for him. He started making a beat with his mouth and snapping his fingers. *"Boom! Snap! Boom! Boom! We got a ball that needs a hoop, we only win if we score, so I guess we better do it some more!"* Everyone smiled and clapped.

His brother clapped the loudest and thought,
"Joshua has an amazing gift."

Song: My Imagination Show

(Joshua's theme song.)
By Dietrich Thompson

(2x) Verse 1:

Oooh, my imagination show
takes me where I want to go,
teach me things I want to know.
There's Noooo, limit to how I grow.
First I learned my ABCs, counting way past 1,2,3

Bridge:

(Why)
The sun comes up.
(I wanna know why)
The flowers grow.
(I wanna know why)
The bees look so busy.
(I wanna know why)
What do they know?
Tell Me! (I wanna know why)
Tell me! (why, why)

Song: I am home
By Dietrich Thompson

Verse 1:

Smelled your good cooking when I walked through the door.
Even with my eyes closed I know what I know.
I am home, Grandma I'm home, I am home, Grandma I'm home.

Verse 2:

How do you know what my favorite foods are?
And, How do you know the song in my heart?
I am home, Grandma I'm home, I am home, Grandma I'm home.

Bridge:

They say home is where the heart is.
You fill it up with all that you give
from the start. So much good food let us live.
All I can say is "thank you."

Verse 3:

Ad Lib

All of your recipes are read from your soul.
Remember every dish, every story you told.
I am home, Grandma I'm home, I am home, Grandma I'm home.

Ad Lib

I am home. I am home
I am home, I am home yeah

Published by Artifex Soul Publishing
914 164th ST SE
Ste B12 #231
Mill Creek, WA 98012

Author: Dietrich Thompson
Illustrations by Randy Knoble

Edited by Dr. Dan Riordan and Mary Riordan.

Summary: A young boy wants to give his brother a gift for his birthday. After some help from his family, we learn his music is an amazing gift.

The illustrations were executed in Adobe Photoshop
The font was set to Maiandra GD

{1.Family-fiction. 2. Problem solving- Fiction. 3.Diversity- Fiction.}

ISBN-13:
978-1532763502

ISBN-10:
1532763506

LCCN:
2016906359

Made in the USA
Middletown, DE
11 May 2019